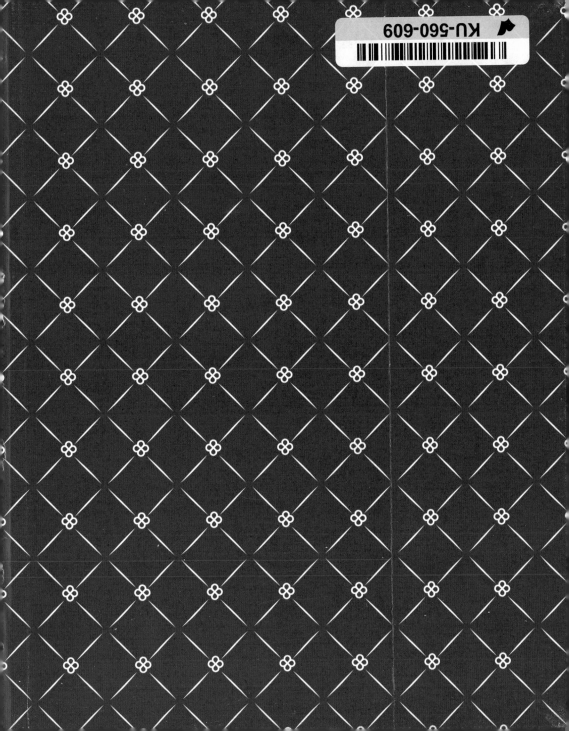

This book belongs to

_____

_____

This edition published by Parragon Books Ltd in 2015

Parragon Books Ltd
Chartist House
15–17 Trim Street
Bath BA1 1HA, UK
www.parragon.com

ISBN 978-1-4748-0641-1

Printed in China

DISNEY MOVIE COLLECTION
A CLASSIC DISNEY STORYBOOK SERIES

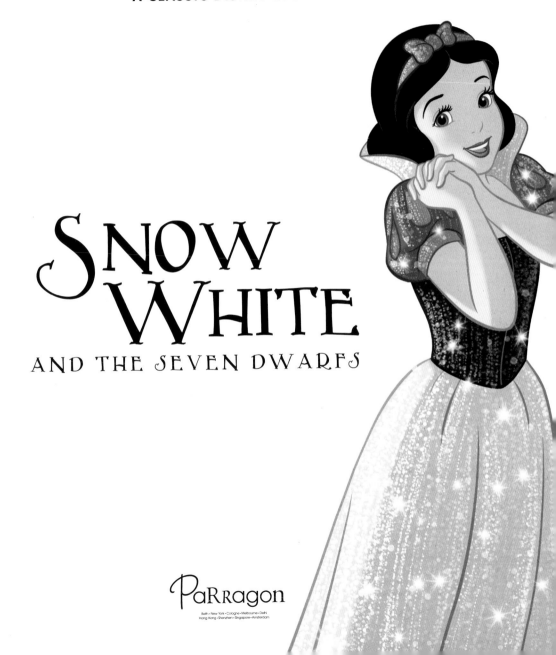

SNOW WHITE
AND THE SEVEN DWARFS

PaRragon
Bath • New York • Cologne • Melbourne • Delhi
Hong Kong • Shenzhen • Singapore • Amsterdam

Once upon a time, there lived a beautiful princess named Snow White. Her stepmother, the Queen, was jealous of Snow White's beauty.

Every day the Queen asked her mirror, "Magic
Mirror on the wall, who is the fairest one of all?"
Each time the mirror would answer, "You are."
But one day the mirror replied, "A lovely maid
I see, who is more fair than thee."
"It's Snow White!" snarled the Queen.

Snow White was in the courtyard, singing as she
went about her chores.

A handsome young prince was riding by and heard
her lovely voice. He climbed the castle wall to find her
but Snow White was shy and ran up to her balcony.

From the courtyard below, the Prince sang
to Snow White and she listened happily.
   She placed a kiss on a friendly dove, who
carried it to the Prince below.

At that very moment, the jealous Queen was plotting against Snow White. She ordered her royal huntsman to take Snow White far into the forest and kill her.

Afraid of angering the Queen, the huntsman took
Snow White into the forest to gather wild flowers.

Snow White kneeled to soothe a baby bird that had
fallen from its nest. "Oh, please don't cry," she said.

As she spoke, the huntsman crept up behind her
with his dagger at the ready.

But the huntsman could not harm the gentle girl.

"Forgive me," he begged. Then he warned Snow White about the Queen's evil plan. "Run away, child, and never come back!"

Snow White fled into the forest. As she
ran, she felt eyes watching her. The trees
seemed to reach out to grab her.

With nowhere left to run, she fell to the
ground and began to cry.

After a while, Snow White looked up and found herself surrounded by forest animals. "Do you know where I can stay?" she asked them.

The friendly animals led Snow White to a tiny cottage
in the woods.

"It's like a doll's house!" said Snow White. She knocked
at the door but no one answered. "Please may I come in?"
she called. Still, there was no reply.

Slowly she stepped inside.

As Snow White wandered through the house, she discovered seven little chairs and seven little beds.

"Seven little children must live here! Let's clean the house and surprise them," the princess suggested. "Then maybe they'll let me stay."

Close by, the seven dwarfs who owned the cottage were busy working in their mine. All day long they dug for diamonds.

At five o'clock it was time to go. Doc led Grumpy, Happy, Sleepy, Sneezy, Bashful and Dopey home, singing and whistling as they went.

When the dwarfs reached their cottage the light was on – someone was in their house! They crept inside and tiptoed upstairs to find someone fast asleep beneath their blankets.

"It's a monster!" whispered one dwarf.

Stepping closer, Doc cried out, "Why, it's a girl!"
The dwarfs gazed at Snow White.
"She's beautiful," Bashful said. "Just like an angel."

Snow White sat up and said, "How do you do?"
She explained to the dwarfs who she was and
what the evil Queen had planned for her.
"Don't send me away," she begged.

"If you let me stay, I'll wash and sew and sweep and cook,"
Snow White promised.

At that the dwarfs shouted, "Hooray! She stays!" And the
happy princess ran to the kitchen to prepare dinner.

The dwarfs rushed downstairs to eat, but Snow White said, "Supper is not quite ready. You'll just have time to wash. Let me see your hands."

They reluctantly showed their dirty hands to Snow White. "Worse than I thought," she said. "March straight outside and wash, or you won't get a bite to eat."

All the dwarfs but one headed to the tub.
"I'd like to see anybody make me wash!"
said Grumpy.

Just as Grumpy spoke, the other dwarfs
pounced on him and dumped him into the
tub. They scrubbed him squeaky-clean.

"You'll pay for this!" growled Grumpy.

Back at the castle, the Queen stood before her
Magic Mirror. "Who is the fairest of them all?" she
asked, as usual. But instead of answering as she had
expected, the mirror told her that Snow White was the
fairest in the land. She was still alive – the huntsman
had lied to her!

The mirror also told the Queen exactly where
Snow White was hiding.

The angry Queen drank a potion that disguised her as an old hag. Then she created a magic apple.

"With one bite of this poisoned apple, Snow White's eyes will close forever," she cackled. "Only a kiss from her true love will wake her!"

Peddler's
Disguise

Formula

Mummy Dust
Black of Night
Old Hag's Cackle
Scream of Fright

Back at the cottage, Snow White and the seven dwarfs were unaware of the Queen's plot. They finished Snow White's delicious dinner and then they sang and danced late into the night.

Even Grumpy joined the fun, thumping away on a pipe organ.

The next morning, Snow White kissed each dwarf goodbye as he marched off to the mine. Dopey even managed to get two kisses!

Doc warned the princess, "The Queen is a sly one. Beware of strangers!"

"Don't let nobody or nothing in the house!" Grumpy added.

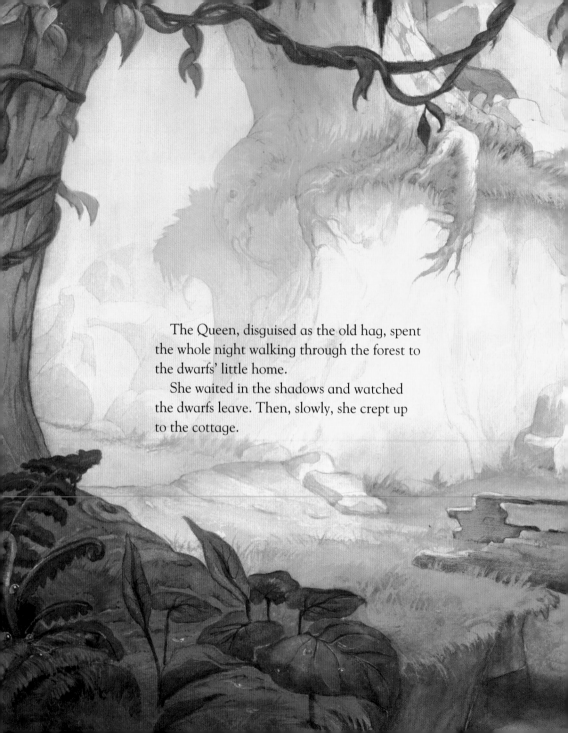

The Queen, disguised as the old hag, spent the whole night walking through the forest to the dwarfs' little home.

She waited in the shadows and watched the dwarfs leave. Then, slowly, she crept up to the cottage.

Snow White was busy making a pie when a shadow fell
over her. She looked up with a gasp and saw the old lady
at the window.

"All alone, my pet?" the Queen asked Snow White.
Then she offered the princess the poisoned apple.

"Go on, have a bite."

Snow White's bird friends knew the old woman was not who she claimed to be. Before Snow White could take the apple, the birds dived at the Queen, pecking her hair and flapping their wings in her face, trying to drive her away.

"Shame on you, frightening an old lady," Snow White scolded the birds. She felt sorry for the old woman and helped her inside the cottage.

The birds and forest animals raced to the
diamond mine to warn the dwarfs. They tugged
on the dwarfs' beards and hats. They pulled
their sleeves and pushed them from behind.
At last, the dwarfs understood.

"The Queen! Snow White!" Doc cried.

"We've got to save her!" Grumpy shouted.

But before the dwarfs could get back to the cottage, Snow White took the poisoned fruit from the old lady and took a single bite.

Snow White fell to the ground, dropping the rest of the apple. "Now I'll be the fairest in the land!" cackled the Queen, as a huge thunderstorm began outside.

The Queen ran from the cottage and out into
the rain. But before she could escape, the seven
dwarfs and all the forest animals came charging at
her through the trees.

"There she goes," cried Grumpy. "After her!"

Thunder boomed overhead and lightning struck all around, but the dwarfs kept on chasing the Queen. They climbed after her and cornered her at the top of a rocky cliff.

"I'll fix you!" she shrieked as she tried to roll an enormous boulder down on top of them.

Suddenly, a bolt of lighting struck the
ledge where the Queen stood!

The rock crumbled beneath her feet and
the evil Queen fell from the cliff and into
the darkness below.

The heartbroken dwarfs built a beautiful bed for the sleeping Snow White and watched over her day and night. Then one day the Prince appeared in the forest clearing.

The handsome Prince had searched far and wide for the girl he had met at the well that morning. When he came to the clearing where Snow White lay, he kneeled down and, with great sorrow, kissed her farewell.

It was Love's First Kiss!

With a soft sigh, Snow White sat up and rubbed her eyes. The Prince shouted with joy and lifted her in his arms. The dwarfs danced and laughed and the woods rang with calls from the happy forest animals. Snow White was alive!

Snow White thanked the dwarfs for all they had done, then kissed each one goodbye, promising to see them again soon. Together, the Prince and Snow White rode off to his castle, where they lived happily ever after.

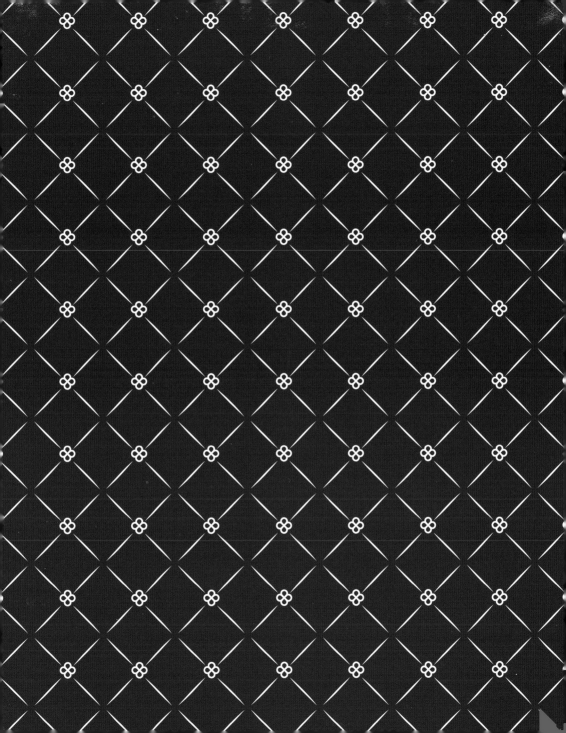

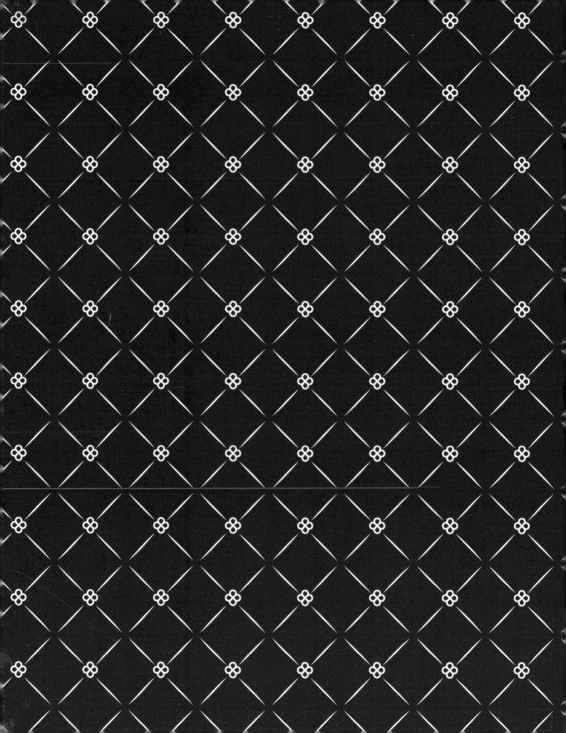